ZONDER**kidz** 1 BEGINNING READING I Can Read!

Fiona Gets the Sniffles

New York Times **Bestselling Illustrator**
Richard Cowdrey
and Donald Wu

D0067201

ZONDER**kidz**
.com

Ah-choo!

Fiona heard a BIG sneeze.

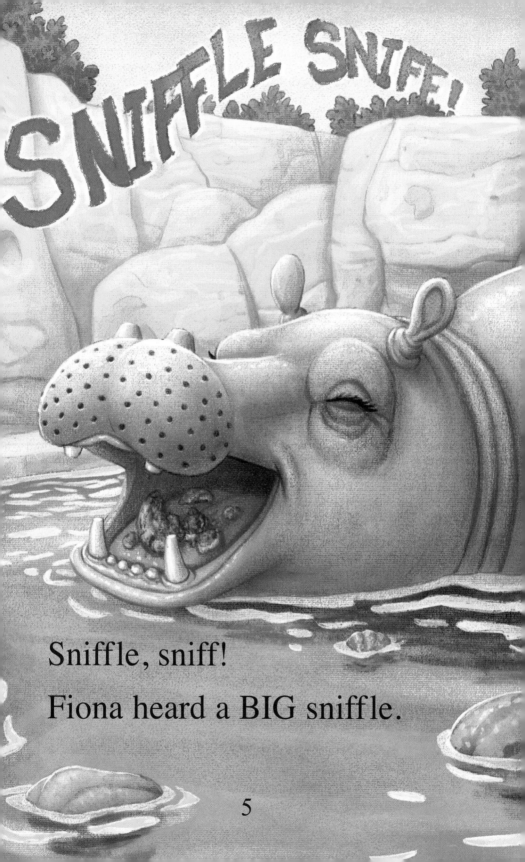

Sniffle, sniff!

Fiona heard a BIG sniffle.

"Mama, did you hear that
sneeze?
Did you hear that sniffle?

I think Mr. Elephant
does not feel well," said Fiona.

"I want to go see Mr. Elephant,"
said Fiona.
"I will help him feel better."

Mama said, "Not today, Fiona.
If you go, you might get
the sneezes and sniffles too."
But Fiona wanted to help!

Fiona went for a walk.
She went to see her animal
friends.

She would ask if they wanted
to help Mr. Elephant feel better.

"Cheetah, I want to help
Mr. Elephant feel better.
What can we do?" asked Fiona.

Cheetah said, "He needs good food.
Hot vegetable soup helps
sneezes and sniffles go away."
But Fiona couldn't get soup.

Mrs. Chicken liked corn.

Corn is good food!

Fiona would ask Mrs. Chicken if she wanted to share some corn with Mr. Elephant!

Cheetah and Fiona went
to see Mrs. Chicken.

"Mrs. Chicken! I want to help
Mr. Elephant feel better.
What can we do?" asked Fiona.

16

"Mr. Elephant needs soft tissues for his nose," said Mrs. Chicken.

Fiona thought about that.

She could not get soft tissues.

But she could bring Mr. Elephant

something soft—Fox!

Fiona, Cheetah, and Mrs. Chicken went to visit Fox.

"Fox, I want to help
Mr. Elephant feel better.
What can we do?" asked Fiona.

"Mr. Elephant needs rest.
Let's sing him a quiet
bedtime song," said Fox.

The animals went to see
Mr. Elephant.
Mr. Elephant still sneezed.
He still sniffled.

"Thank you for coming to
see me. But I need rest now,"
said Mr. Elephant.

Fiona, Cheetah, Mrs. Chicken,
and Fox waved good-bye.
They went home.

On the way home,
Fiona sniffled.
Fiona sneezed.

Ah-choo!

Mama heard a BIG sneeze.

Sniffle, sniff!
Mama heard a BIG sniffle.

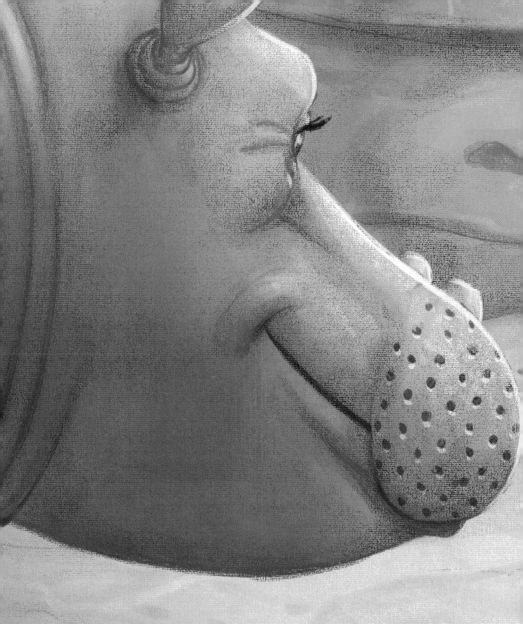

Fiona said, "You were right, Mama.
I went to help Mr. Elephant.
He has the sniffles. Now, I do too."

Mama said, "I am proud of you.
You helped your friend.
Now I will help you."

Mama got Fiona good food
and soft tissues.
Fiona had a good rest too.

Fiona felt much better!